HOW MANY MICE?

MICHAEL GARLAND

Dutton Children's Books

DUTTON CHILDREN'S BOOKS
A division of Penguin Young Readers Group

Published by the Penguin Group
Penguin Group (USA) Inc., 375 Hudson Street, New York, New York 10014, U.S.A. • Penguin Group (Canada), 90 Eglinton Avenue East, Suite 700, Toronto, Ontario, Canada M4P 2Y3 (a division of Pearson Penguin Canada Inc.) • Penguin Books Ltd, 80 Strand, London WC2R 0RL, England • Penguin Ireland, 25 St Stephen's Green, Dublin 2, Ireland (a division of Penguin Books Ltd) • Penguin Group (Australia), 250 Camberwell Road, Camberwell, Victoria 3124, Australia (a division of Pearson Australia Group Pty Ltd) • Penguin Books India Pvt Ltd, 11 Community Centre, Panchsheel Park, New Delhi - 110 017, India • Penguin Group (NZ), Cnr Airborne and Rosedale Roads, Albany, Auckland 1310, New Zealand (a division of Pearson New Zealand Ltd) • Penguin Books (South Africa) (Pty) Ltd, 24 Sturdee Avenue, Rosebank, Johannesburg 2196, South Africa • Penguin Books Ltd, Registered Offices: 80 Strand, London WC2R 0RL, England

Library of Congress Cataloging-in-Publication Data

Garland, Michael, date.
How many mice? / Michael Garland.—1st ed.   p. cm.
Summary: Ten hungry mice set out on a mission to find some food, facing hazards
and dangers along the way.
ISBN 978-0-525-47833-1 (hardcover) [1. Mice—Fiction. 2. Counting.] I. Title.
PZ7.G18413Ho 2007 [E]—dc22 2006024468

Published in the United States by Dutton Children's Books,
a division of Penguin Young Readers Group
345 Hudson Street, New York, New York 10014
www.penguin.com/youngreaders

Designed by Jason Henry and Abby Kuperstock
Manufactured in China • First Edition
1 3 5 7 9 10 8 6 4 2

To my favorite math teacher,

Rick Somma

Can you count to ten?

Ten hungry mice set off from home to gather food for a meal.

They found some cherries under the old cherry tree, one for each.

But as the mice crossed the meadow, three greedy crows swooped down and stole four of their cherries.

How many cherries do the mice have now?

There was not enough food for the mice, so they crept into a garden and picked two big red tomatoes.

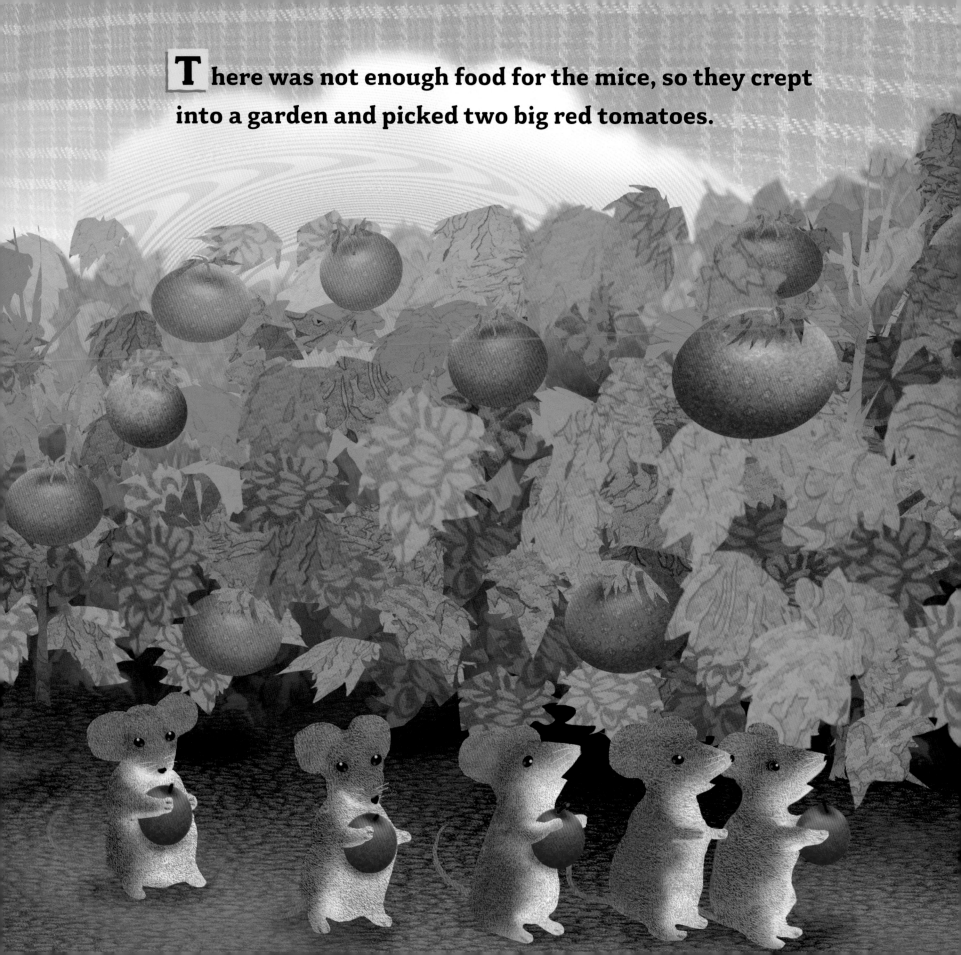

How many pieces of food do the mice have?

Next the mice searched the cornfield. They discovered four ears of corn lying on the ground.

Can you count all the pieces of food?

On the way back home, as they were crossing a stream, a fish leaped out of the water. Splash!

How many pieces of food fell into the stream?

Some of the mice were almost washed away.

Can you count the mice who have no food?

How many pieces of food do the mice have now?

Next the mice went to the old oak tree, and there they collected seven acorns. They had plenty of food now, so they headed down the path for home.

Suddenly, a fox jumped from the bushes. The mice were so scared, they ran for their lives!

How many pieces of food did the mice drop?

The ten mice escaped, but they lost some of their food.
No matter, the farmer's field was on the way home.

Can you find the mouse who has no food?

The mice dug up three carrots. As they marched away, they had no idea that someone was watching them.

How many cherries do the mice have now?

How many acorns do the mice have now?

Suddenly, a great horned owl swooped down from the sky, scattering the mice in every direction.

Luckily, all the mice escaped. One by one the mice returned home after their adventure.

How many pieces of food did the mice bring home?

At last they were back home safely. If each mouse eats one thing, how many mice will it take to eat all the food?

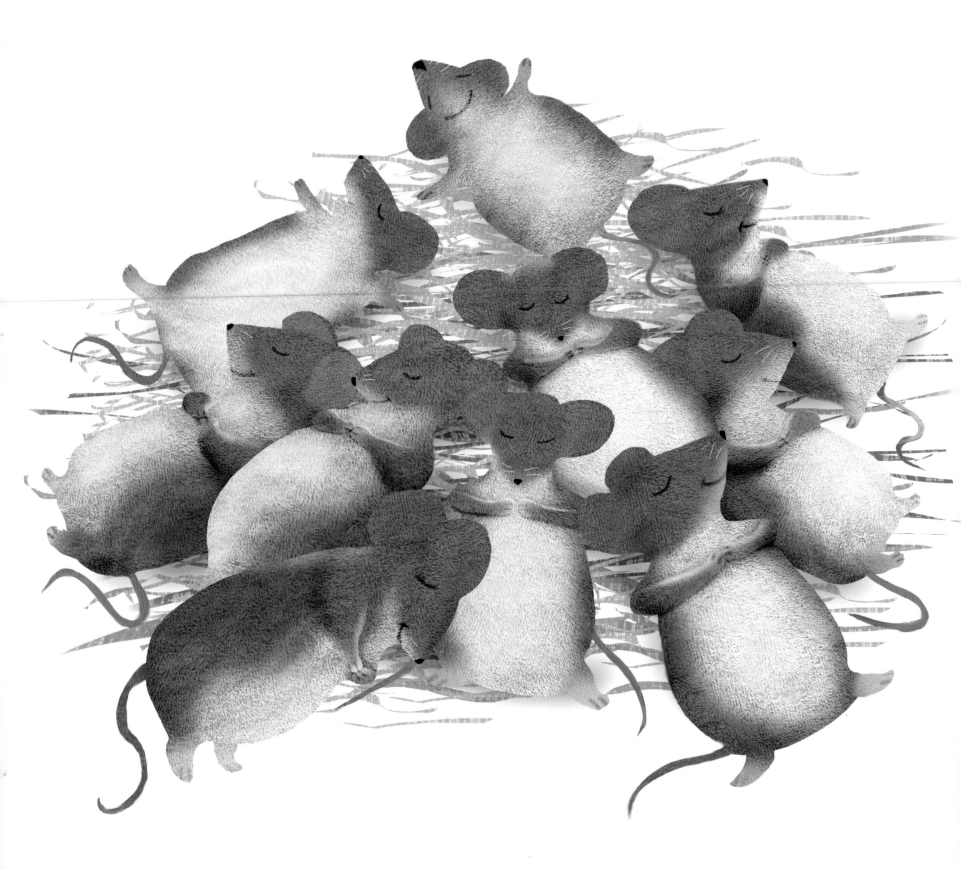